Magnets

Sandy Sepehri

Bethany, Missouri

Photo Credits:
Cover © Harry Hu; Title Page © Michael Chamberlin; Page 5 © Dany Farina; Page 6 © Matthew Cole; Page 7 © Image 100; Page 9 © Carolina Smith; Page 16 © ARTEKI; Page 17 © PMSI; Page 18 © Armentrout; Page 19 © Lebedinski Vladislav Evgenievitch, Donald R. Swartz; Page 20 © Michelle D. Milliman; Page 21 © Chris Ryan, Stephen Aaron Rees; Page 22 © Athewma Athewma

Cataloging-in-Publication Data

Sepehri, Sandy
Magnets / Sandy Sepehri. — 1st ed.
p. cm. — (Physical science)

Includes bibliographical references and index.
Summary: Text and photographs introduce the physical science of magnets and magnetism, including what they are and how they play a part in everyday life.
ISBN-13: 978-1-4242-1415-0 (lib. bdg. : alk. paper)
ISBN-10: 1-4242-1415-7 (lib. bdg. : alk. paper)
ISBN-13: 978-1-4242-1505-8 (pbk. : alk. paper)
ISBN-10: 1-4242-1505-6 (pbk. : alk. paper)

1. Magnets—Juvenile literature. 2. Magnetism—Juvenile literature. [1. Magnets. 2. Magnetism.]
I. Sepehri, Sandy. II. Title. III. Series.
QC757.5.S47 2007
538—dc22

First edition

802 N. 41st Street, P.O. Box 505
Bethany, MO 64424, U.S.A.
Printed in China
Library of Congress Control Number: 2006940890

Table of Contents

Magnets, Not Magic

Why don't the paper clips fall? Is it magic? No. It's magnets! Inside the paper clip holder is a magnet. The magnet holds the paper clips.

Magnet

Magnets hold some metal things. These things are usually made of steel, iron, nickel, or even other magnets.

Some refrigerator doors are made of steel. Magnets stick to steel.

Magnets come in many shapes and sizes. **Magnetism** is useful.

Support Our Troops

Hold two magnets close together and you can feel a pull or push between them. You are feeling **magnetic forces**.

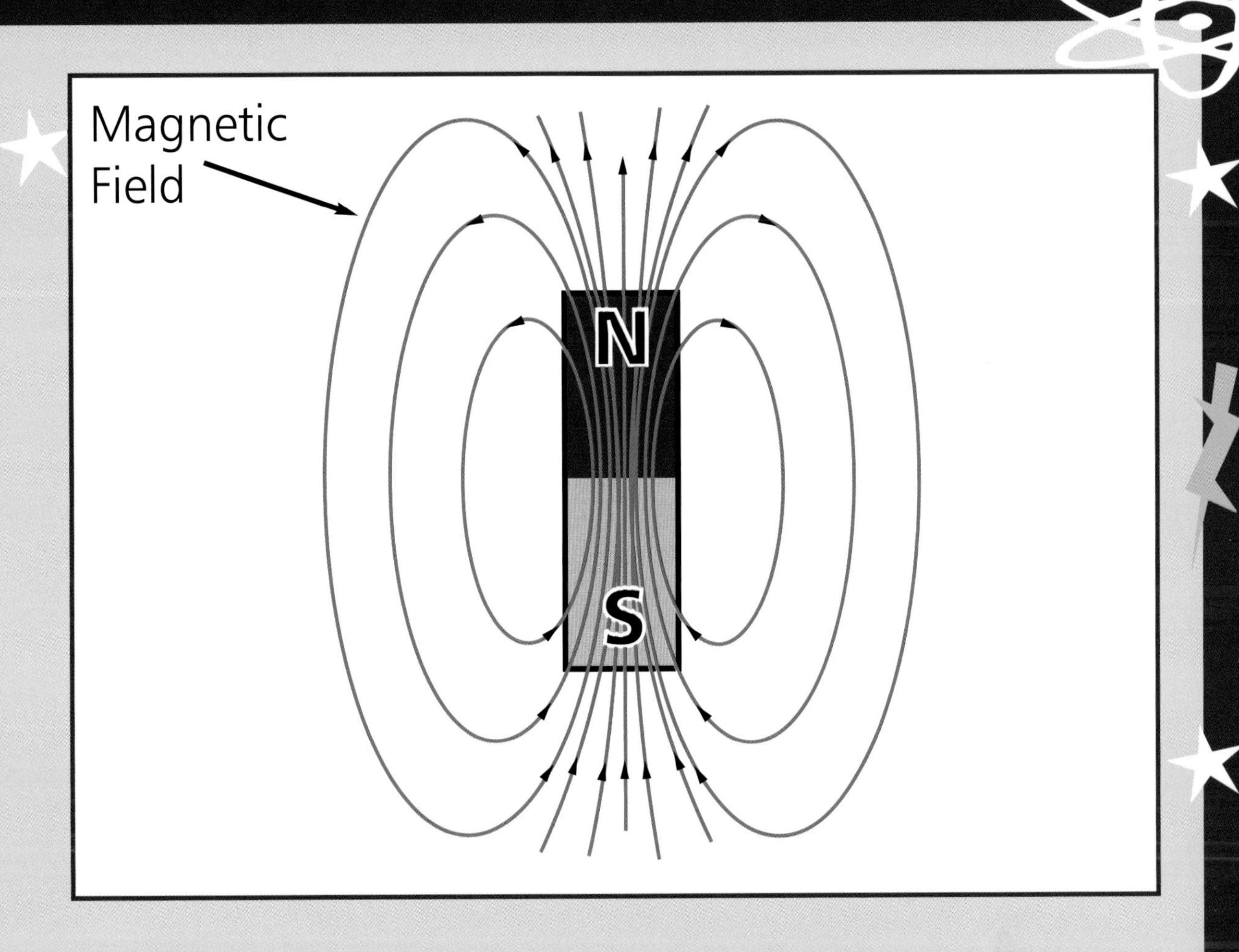

Magnetic fields are magnetic forces around magnets.

The Earth Magnet

The Earth is like a giant magnet, with its own magnetic field around it. Just like the Earth, all magnets have a north and south pole.

The Earth's Magnetic Field

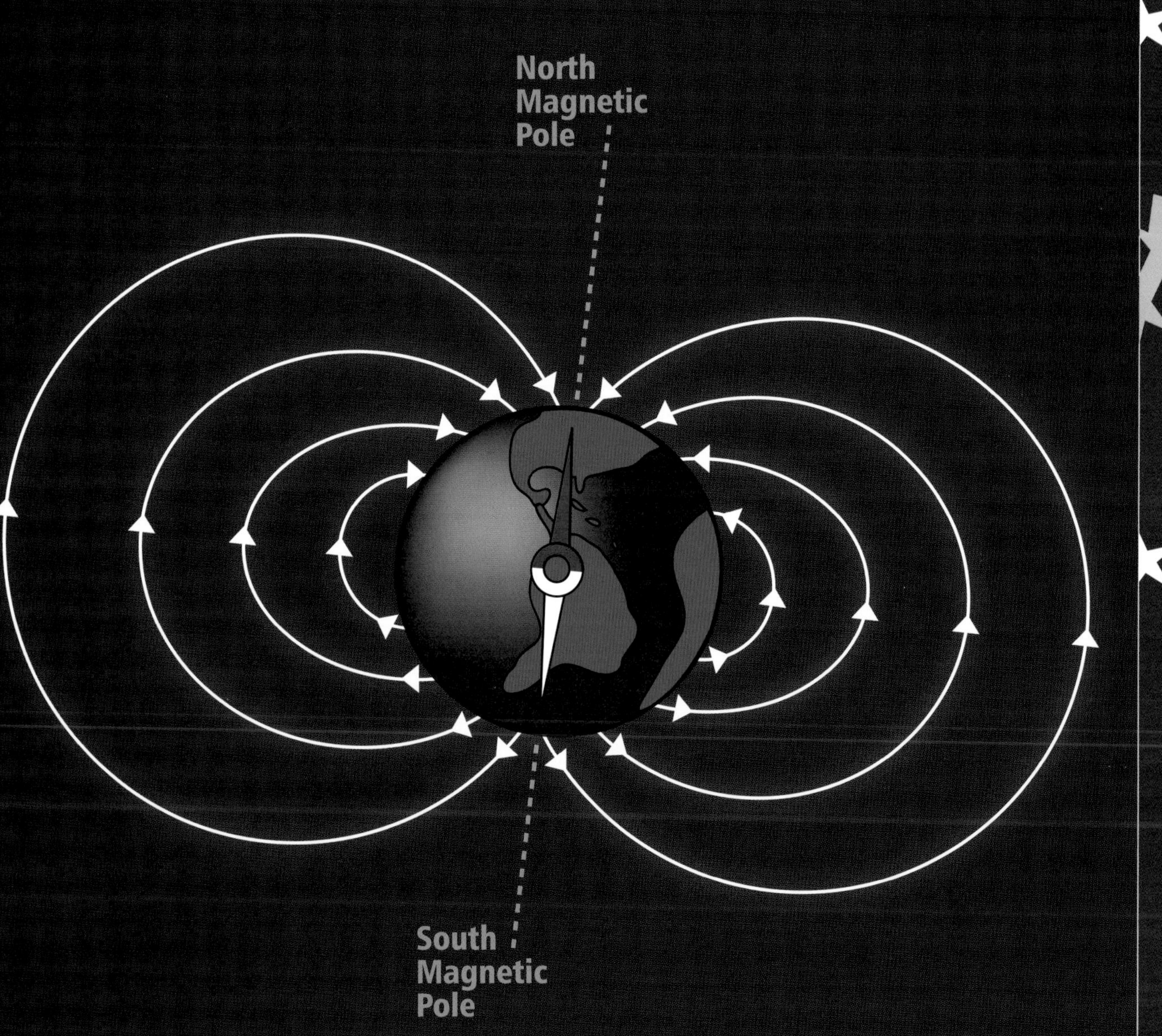

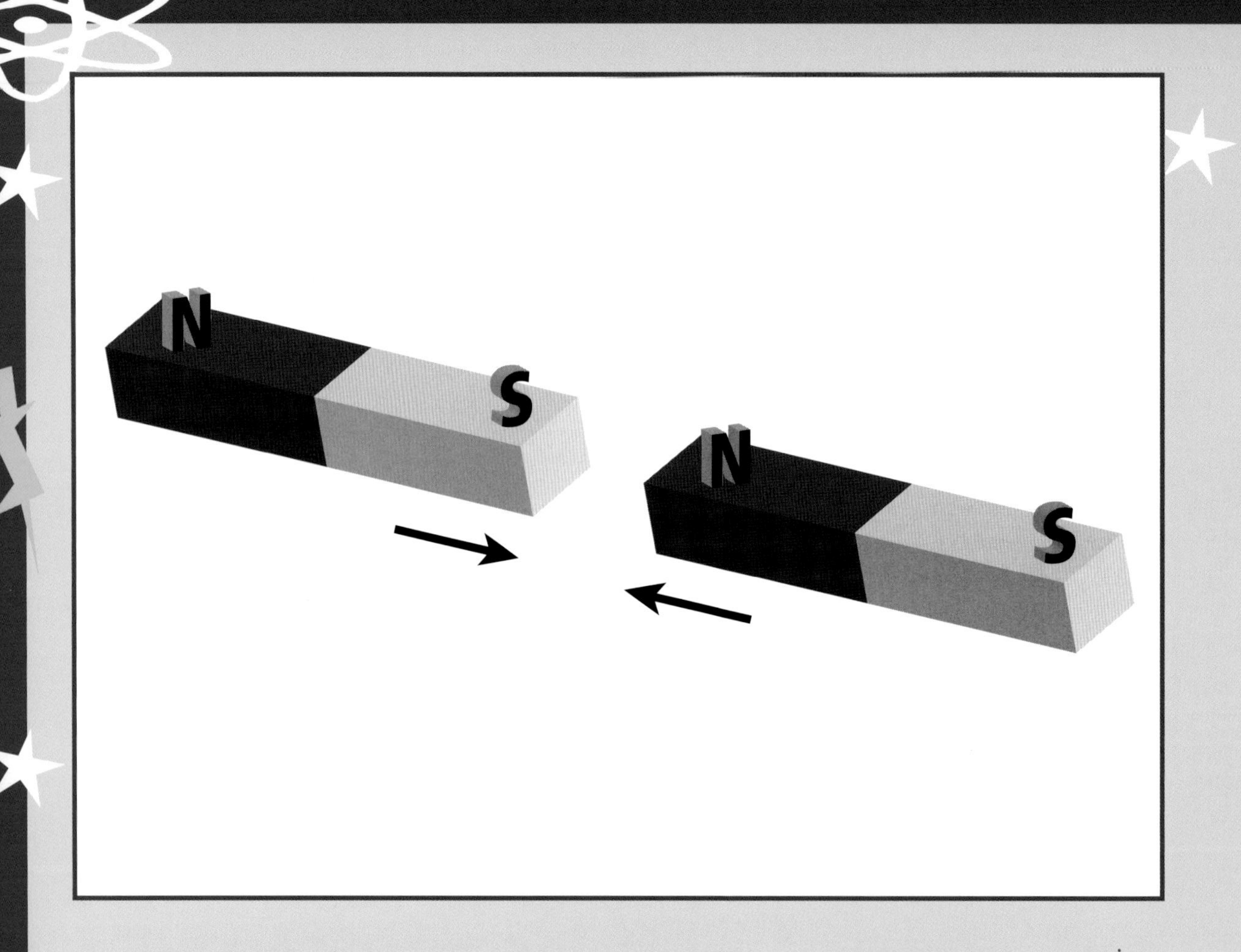

North poles are pulled toward south poles.

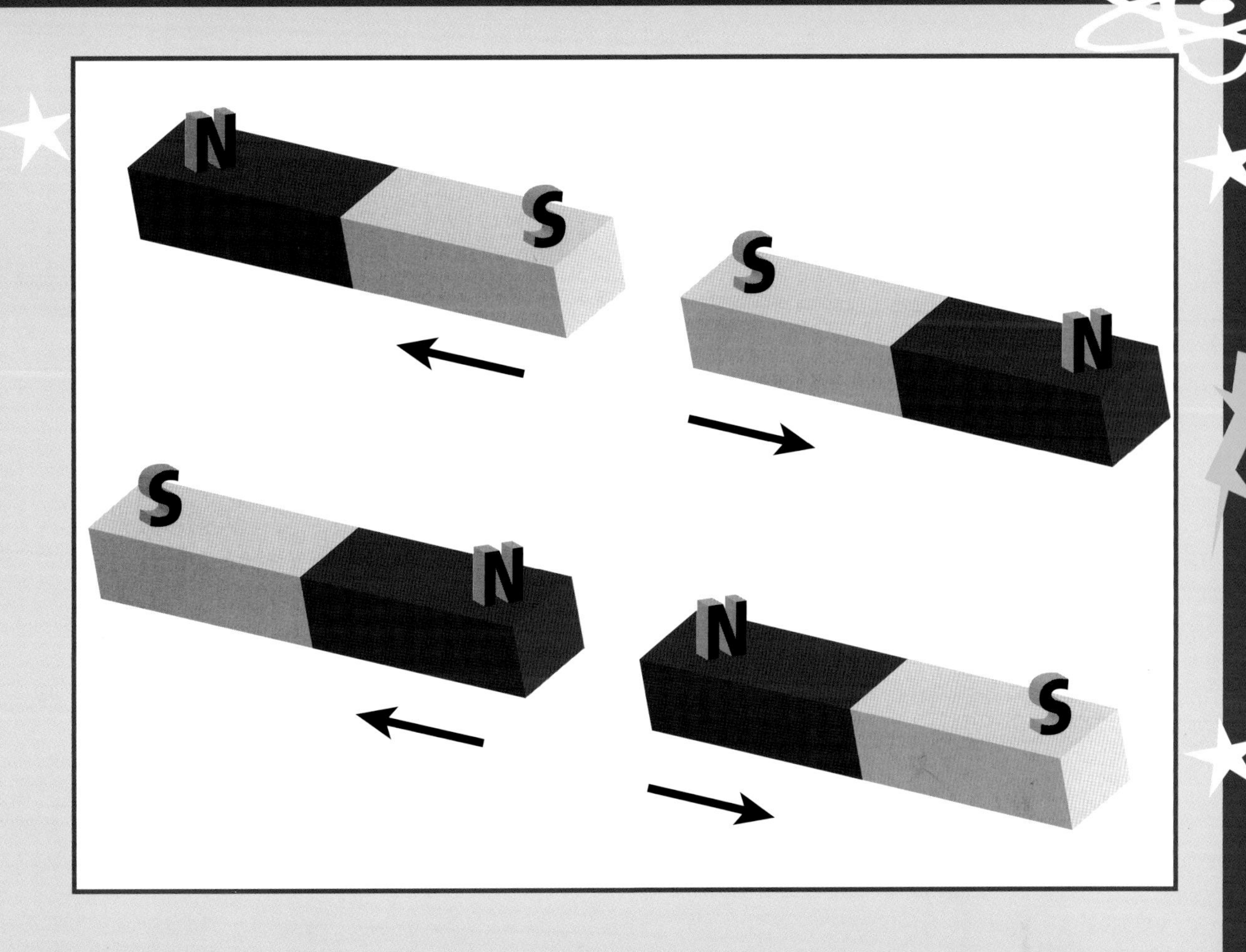

North poles push away from north poles, and south poles push away from south poles.

Magnets at Work

A compass uses magnets. The magnetized red pointer of a compass always lines up with the Earth's north magnetic pole. A compass helps us go the right direction.

Magnetic North

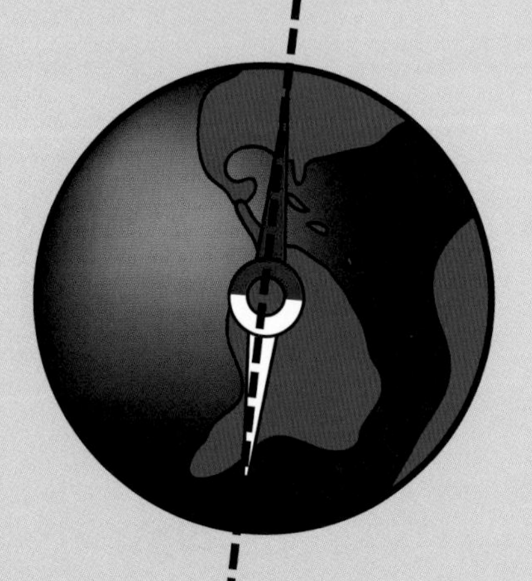

Magnetic South

Magnetic North

Magnetic South

Magnets help sort metals at recycling centers.

Some magnets use electricity to help them do their job. These are called **electromagnets**.

Magnets help make the electricity we use in our homes.

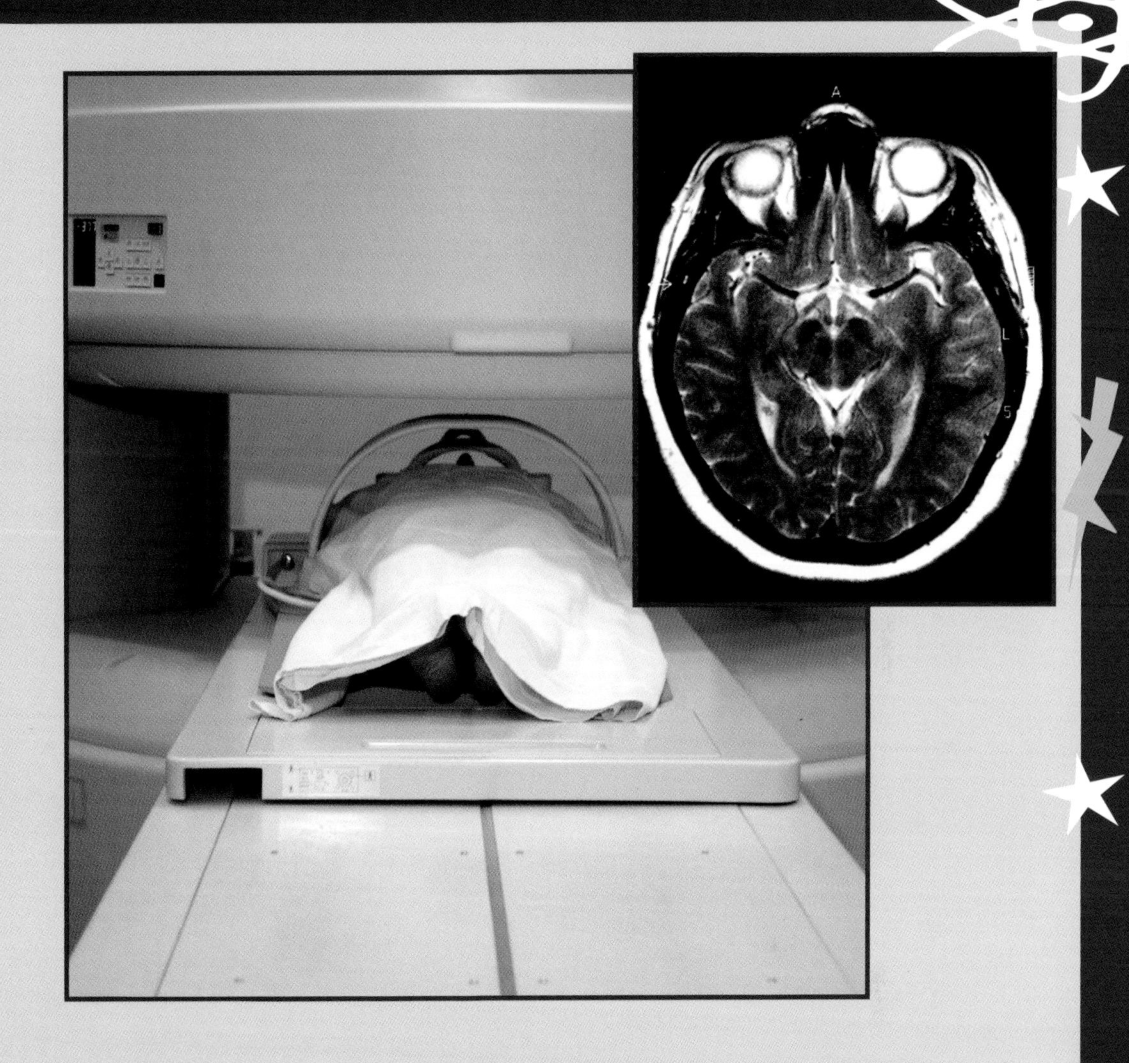

Magnets help doctors find problems. A magnetic resonance imaging machine takes pictures inside the body.

Magnets have important jobs and simple jobs. Life would be very different without magnets!

Glossary

magnetism (MAG neh tis em) — the properties of a magnet

magnetic forces (mag NEH tic FORS es) — the pulling or pushing that happens in magnetic fields

magnetic fields (mag NEH tic FEELDS) — the spaces all around magnets where the forces of the magnets act

electromagnet (i lek truh MAG nit) — a magnet powered by electricity

Index

FURTHER READING

Olien, Rebecca. *Magnets.* Bridgestone Books, 2003.
Parker, Steve. *Electricity and Magnetism.* Chelsea House, 2005.
Rosinsky, Natalie. *Magnets: Pulling and Pushing.* Picture Window Books, 2003.

WEBSITES TO VISIT

Because Internet links change so often, Fitzgerald Books has developed an online list of websites related to the subject of this book. This site is updated regularly. Please use this link to access the list: www.fitzgeraldbookslinks.com/ps/mag

ABOUT THE AUTHOR

Sandy Sepehri is an honors graduate from the University of Central Florida. She has authored several children's books and is a columnist for a parents' magazine.